The Mummy's Finger

Written by
Ian MacDonald

Illustrated by Charlie Clough

First Published
May 2009 in Great Britain by

PUBLISHING

© Ian MacDonald 2009

A CIP record for this work is available from the British Library

ISBN-10: 1-905637-77-2
ISBN-13: 978-1-905637-77-5

Typeset by Educational Printing Services Limited

Educational Printing Services Limited
Unit 6, Glenfield Park 2, Northrop Avenue, Blackburn BB1 5QH
Telephone: (01254) 686500   Fax: (01254) 686501
E-mail: enquiries@eprint.co.uk   Website: www.eprint.co.uk

CONTENTS

Prologue:
The Story of Osiris

Once there was a King of Egypt whose name was Osiris. He was a good king and ruled wisely over the land. He had a beautiful wife called Isis, who loved him dearly. But Osiris had a wicked brother called Seth. Seth had the heart and soul of a beast and he was jealous of his brother's power. One day Seth held a grand party.

When everyone had arrived, he brought out a great wooden chest which he had made with his own hands. It was very beautiful and all the guests admired it.

"Anyone who can fit perfectly inside may be its owner," said Seth. One by one they all tried it out, but they were either too large or too small to fit. But when Osiris stepped in and lay down, it was a perfect fit... just as Seth knew it would be! Seth slammed the lid and nailed it down. Then he took the chest and put it into the Nile. But brave Isis sailed her boat down the river and brought back the body of her husband from the waters of the Nile. When Seth heard what had happened, he flew into a rage and he went to seek out his brother's body. Finding him in the royal palace, he took

his sword and cut Osiris into fourteen
pieces and scattered them far and wide all
across the land of Egypt. But patient, loving
Isis searched for many days. She did not
rest until she had found every single piece
and had put his body back together. And so
Osiris was able to go on into the afterlife,
where he waited for his loyal wife to be with
him once more.

The Mummy Room

"... so Osiris was able to go on into the afterlife, where he waited for his loyal wife to be with him once more," said the museum guide.

"Awww, what a lovely story," said Becky Thomson.

"Lovely?" said Chaz, "having all your bits

and bobs chopped off and chucked all over the place!"

Becky Thomson made a sulky face.

"Now, now, children," said Mrs Bagshaw, frowning, "let our guide finish."

"Well," smiled the guide, "that story from Ancient Egypt helps us understand what they believed about life and death. Can you think what it tells us?"

"Don't go climbing into boxes that you don't know?" suggested Scott.

"True love always wins in the end," twittered Millie Albright.

All the boys groaned.

"Well, no," said the guide, weakly. "It tells us that the Egyptians believed that their bodies must be preserved so that they could enter into the next world."

"What's pre-versed?" said Scott.

"Preserved ... to last for thousands of years," corrected the guide, looking at her watch. Now we can go and see some of the mummies before lunch. Follow me, please."

At the mention of lunch everyone perked up.

"Wow! Best school outing I've been on," said Ryan.

"Yeah, can't wait to see the mummies," said Freddie.

"What about the daddies?" laughed Chaz.

"Hah, hah, very funny," said Owen, rolling his eyes. This only made the two other boys giggle even more.

The children crowded round the glass case. Owen pushed to the front for the best view. Freddie and Chaz pushed in beside him, nudging Becky Thomson out of the way.

"Cor," hissed Freddie, "look at the old bloke in the bandages."

"That's a mummy," whispered Owen.

Freddie and Chaz giggled, remembering their joke. Owen ignored them.

"... and this mummy is nearly four thousand years old. His name is Chum Ra Otep and he was ruler in Ancient Egypt in the Old Kingdom ...," the guide's voice droned on.

In the glass case was a body of a man wrapped from head to toe in bandages. And, under the ancient cloth: a face, a nose, a mouth and two closed eyes. The mummy's arms were folded across his chest, every finger perfect – you could count them.

Someone behind Freddie pushed closer to get a better look. Freddie pushed back but only succeeded in stumbling against the glass. Mrs Bagshaw frowned. Freddie looked at the mummy's hand.

And one of the fingers fell off!

Sweets

No one else had noticed.

Freddie crouched down to get a better look.

Everyone else was busy watching the guide. She held up what looked like a small doll. It held a tiny bow and arrow. "This is called a *shabti*. It is a wooden carving of a warrior in a Pharaoh's army."

The finger was just lying there, like a shrivelled sausage.

"The *shabti* would be placed in the pharaoh's tomb to come alive and serve him when he passed into the next world."

Freddie pressed his own finger to the glass. The mummy's finger was almost exactly the same size.

"But, he could only go on to the afterlife if his body had been preserved with nothing missing. This ancient spell was found written on his tomb. It goes like this: *'Oh keep my body from the destroyer. May him who is the keeper of my heart, my tongue, my liver...'* "

"Miss, I feel sick," moaned Becky Thomson, going a bit green.

"Never mind. Soon be lunchtime," grinned Abbie Stokes.

"*May he hold my bones and keep them for the time which is to come ...*"

Freddie looked down.

The finger was *outside* the glass!

He gulped and looked around him. Still no one was looking. They were still listening to the guide. He looked down again. It was still there. Small and grey, curled up against the glass like a sleeping mouse.

He slowly stretched out a hand.

Two fingers ... worlds apart ... almost touching. Freddie knelt down. His own fingers closed gently around the mummy's finger.

"Freddie! What's that in your hand?"

"Nothing, Miss!"

Freddie jerked to his feet, thrusting his hands behind him.

"Is that a tube of sweets you're holding?"

"No, I haven't got sweets, Miss, honest!"

Freddie could feel the finger pressing into his sweaty palm. It felt cold, like stone.

The other children were staring now. Freddie looked around, wildly. Owen was standing in front of him, his back turned towards him. His pocket was slightly open. It looked like a tiny mouse hole.

"Freddie, you know you're not allowed to bring sweets on a school trip."

"Miss, it's ... I haven't got any sweets, Miss."

Now Owen's pocket looked like a small cave.

"Give it to me ... now!"

"What, Miss?"

"You know what, Freddie. I shan't ask you again. What have you got in your hand?"

"I haven't got nothing, Miss!"

The pocket gaped like a train tunnel.

Mrs Bagshaw was now walking towards Freddie.

He held up two empty hands.

"Look, Miss! Nothing, Miss!"

SNAKES AND SHUDDERS

"You did what?!" spluttered Owen.

"Well ... you shouldn't have such big pockets," mumbled Freddie.

"He's right there, Owen. You have got big pockets. I mean they're like ..."

"Can we stop discussing my trousers. This ... donkey-brain's just gone and put a ..."

"Keep your voice down," said Freddie, scrunching back in his train seat.

"... put an old Pharaoh's finger in *my* pocket," hissed Owen.

"Let's have a look, then," said Chaz, leaning over.

"Not here! Not on the train!" said Freddie, anxiously. "What if old Baggy-Pants finds out?"

"Behind here, then." Chaz picked up a large newspaper from the seat opposite, and pretended to read. Mrs Bagshaw looked across and raised an eyebrow. She had never seen Chaz read anything in his life, except the football team list on Mr Farley's notice board.

"Let's have a look, then."

Owen wriggled on the seat as he fished in his pocket. Carefully, he held out the strange object between finger and thumb. All three peered closely. The finger was slightly bent. It was dull grey and papery, and looked like it might crumble to dust at any moment. At one end the bandage had come away a little, showing a glimpse of white skin... four thousand years old!

"What are we going to do?" said Chaz, keeping his head down. "Chuck it out the window?"

"Good idea," said Freddie, and reached over.

Owen pushed him away. "Are you mad? What about the story?"

"What are you on about?" said Chaz.

"You know...the Pharaoh can't go into the next life with one of his...bits missing."

"What, you think the old bloke's going to come looking for his finger?"

His voice trailed off as the train slowly stopped at the next station.

Chaz lowered the newspaper a little and the boys peered over the top.

Staring in at them from outside the train window was an eyeless head wrapped in bandages. Two hands reached out, blindly searching. A black snake curled about the creature's leg. Owen stood up to have a closer look. The train doors hissed open.

At the foot of the poster, in large red letters, it said:

> # REVENGE OF THE MUMMY
> ## IN CINEMAS NOW!
> ## DARE YOU SEE IT?

The doors shuddered closed and the train pulled away.

Owen held the finger tight, hardly daring to breathe. He looked round at the crowded carriage. He was sure everyone was watching. Nearby a girl sat falling asleep, her braided-hair nodding like a bag of snakes. On the seat opposite, a large-nosed man was reading a book in another language. The words were just squiggles, so many snakes slithering over white paper. A small boy was putting his fingers to his mouth. He pulled his finger out, and a long, wriggling, black shape came snaking from between dark lips.

Owen felt the sweat begin to run down his back as he settled back in his seat.

"If you are going to mess about with that liquorice, I'm going to take it away," said the small boy's mother, yanking the boy's arm. The snake-haired girl looked up. Big-nose closed his book and stood up to leave.

Chaz loosened his collar and wiped the sweat from his forehead. Freddie climbed up on the seat to open a window. The train clattered around a bend. Freddie stumbled sideways. He stuck out his foot to save himself, and plunged it into Owen's lap. With a howl of pain, Owen clapped his hands to his trousers. Something dropped from his hands and tumbled to the floor.

"Eeeek! A mouse!" screamed a woman.

Several of the women and a large man in baggy shorts, were already standing on the seats. A man in a dark suit reached down. But Chaz was there first.

Chaz grabbed the finger. Everyone in the carriage began to clap. Chaz grinned and pulled off his baseball cap to take a bow.

A lady stepped forward and put some money in it. Soon his cap was full of coins and notes.

Chaz started to count the money but stopped when he caught sight of Mrs Bagshaw striding towards him like an angry bull. The train slowed and the doors hissed open.

"Come on!" Chaz dived for the doors, pulling Freddie behind him. Owen followed and the doors clattered shut behind them.

"What now?" said Freddie.

"We've got to get back to the museum," said Owen, "and return the mummy's finger."

Professor Chadwick

It was beginning to get dark.

The three boys stood peering through the railings of an enormous iron gate.

Owen took out the little card that he had in his pocket.

```
┌─────────────────────────────────────────────┐
│                                               │
│   Prof. Stanton Chadwick          ⌑ ⌐         │
│                                    ⟁ ⌡         │
│   Professor of Egyptology          ⌐ ⌐         │
│                                               │
│   The Towers                       ⌐ ⌡         │
│   Warrenside Avenue                ⌐ ⌐         │
│   London                           ⌐ ⌡         │
│   W1 3BG                           ⌐ ⌐         │
│                                               │
└─────────────────────────────────────────────┘
```

They had found the card mysteriously
stuffed under a five pound note in Chaz's
cap. Some of the money had been spent on
train fares and a street map. Now they
squinted at the great black shape of the
house at the end of a bramble-covered path.

It was more like a castle than a house.
Turrets and towers pointed into the
darkening sky and ivy crawled up the walls.
There were no lights on anywhere.

"There's no one in," said Freddie. "We'll come back tomorrow, eh?"

Owen made no reply.

"Anyway, how do we get in, shouldn't there be a bell or something?" said Chaz.

As if the gate had listened, it slowly creaked open. Owen and Chaz stepped inside. Freddie followed close behind. They walked up the path, stepping over the creeping ivy, and climbed the steps to the front door. The great black iron door knocker was in the shape of a snake. Nervously, Owen reached up and gave three loud taps. There was no answer. He knocked again. This time the door opened a little, with a sound like someone sighing.

"Follow me," said Owen, stepping inside.

"I'll wait here and keep a look-out, shall I?" whispered Freddie.

Chaz grabbed Freddie by his shirt
collar and hauled him through the doorway.

It was dark inside. A few candles cast
flickering shadows over a great staircase
which curved upwards into the gloom. A
sound from above made them look up.

Freddie took a step backwards.

There was somebody at the top of the
stairs. A shadowy figure in the candlelight.
He was no taller than any of the boys. He
held a candlestick in one hand.

"Ah, you've come at last," said a voice.

"It's him ... from the train," whispered
Chaz, "the man with the book."

"How did you know we were coming?" called out Owen.

The man laughed, a sound like fingernails on glass. "I knew you would not refuse my invitation. Now, come up here where I can see you. "

The boys looked at each other and
started up the stairs.

At the top they followed the man along a dark passageway until they came to a large room. At the doorway the little man paused and turned to face the three boys. White hair sprouted wildly from under a sort of round hat and a pair of round glasses perched on his large nose. He looked more like an owl than a man.

"Now, let me introduce myself. I am Professor Stanton Chadwick, Professor of Egyptology and expert in ancient languages. I think I might be able to help with your little problem."

They went inside the room. On every wall, shelves were stacked high with old books. A long wooden table was covered with more books, and rolls of yellowing paper were bundled together, tied with string.

Sitting down, the little man picked up a large leather book and blew a cloud of dust from the cover.

34

Curious, the boys stepped nearer to see.

"Now, let me see," said the Professor, running a bony finger over the page, "Egyptians ... Pharaohs ... scribes ... incantations ... spells. Ah, here we are ...The Book of the Dead."

"What's all them squiggly things?" whispered Freddie.

"Hieroglyphics," breathed Owen, "Egyptian writing."

"What did you mean back there," asked Chaz, "about the little problem?"

"Come, come, let's not play games," said

the Professor. "You have the finger of Chum Ra Otep. I saw it on the train. I knew it immediately. He will want it back, you know."

"What for?" said Chaz. "He doesn't play the piano, does he?"

"I don't think you understand," said the Professor, peering over his glasses. "If the Pharaoh does not get his finger back, he cannot find rest in the afterlife. I promise you, as sure as the sun rises...he will come."

Jars and Bottles

"Now, I'm forgetting my manners. Peppermint tea, anyone?"

The Professor left the room, leaving the book open on the table.

Owen ran his fingers over the lines of pictures. They meant nothing, just squiggles, dots and pictures. How could this be a language? Then he spotted the tiny writing at the bottom of the page.

"Look, it's translated. There, see?" he said.

"May he hold my bones and keep them for the time which is to come...and he who steals my bones shall suffer the death of a thousand..."

"A thousand *what*?" said Chaz.

"The word's not clear ... wait, here's the picture above. It's a kind of crab thing ... with a squiggly line ... maybe a tail ..."

"Scorpions!" said Chaz and Freddie, together.

"Still," began Freddie, "we haven't got anyone's bones, have we?"

"What do you think is inside that finger then, pea-brain?" said Owen.

But Freddie was not listening.

He was staring at something on the wall.

"What?" said Chaz.

"L ... look," stammered Freddie, pointing.

Owen turned. On the shelves behind him were rows of jars and bottles of every shape and size.

Owen went over and peered into the nearest jar. There was something floating. A dead mouse. He examined the others in turn: a big toe ... some human hair ... a row of teeth ... an eyeball ...

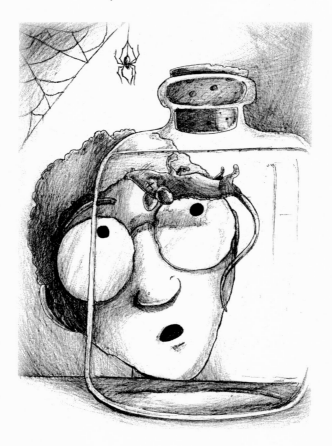

"What's it all for?" asked Freddie.

"He's a professor, isn't he?" said Chaz. "I expect he does experiments 'n' stuff."

"We've got to get out of here. Now!" said Owen, scrambling to his feet.

"What's the hurry?" said Chaz.

"Yeah," said Freddie, "you wanted to come here in the first place!"

"Don't you see?" said Owen. "This place is full of Egyptian body bits. If you're out looking for your lost finger ... this is the first place you'd come."

The boys looked at Owen.

Then at each other.

"RUN!"

Leaping down the steps two or three at a time, they came to the front door.

"Wait!" shouted Owen, grabbing Freddie by the collar.

"What now?"

"I've left it behind, the finger. Wait here."

Owen charged back up the stairs, hoping the Professor would not re-appear. He grabbed the finger and started racing back. When he reached the top of the staircase again, the others were there.

"What are you doing up here?" gasped Owen.

"There's a ... a ...," stammered Freddie.

"It's a ... m ... mum ...," joined in Chaz.

Owen looked.

Something was coming up the stairs.

It rocked clumsily from side-to-side as it came.

It was wrapped in bandages from head to foot.

Two bulges on the creature's chest, and a few wisps of long, white hair, gave Owen a clue. The sand-coloured handbag dangling from one arm was a dead giveaway!

"Aaaaargh! It's the mummy's missus!"

The boys all tried to run at once. Freddie caught his foot in the carpet and fell. Chaz and Owen stumbled over him. In a flurry of arms and legs they tumbled into the nearest room and slammed the door.

"What does she want?" stammered Freddie.

"The finger of course," said Owen. "Don't you remember the story? The Pharaoh's wife will come looking for her husband's ... lost bits." Then he flapped at his pockets. "Oh no! I must have dropped it."

Opening the door a little, the boys peered out. They poked their heads round the door frame.

The mummy woman was standing at the top of the stairs. She was tugging a piece of bandage that had caught on a nail. She looked up and saw the boys.

With a scream of rage, she pulled hard but, losing her balance she began to fall, flailing her thin arms and clawing the air. Her bandages began to unwind like a toilet roll as she spun down the stairs.

A cloud of white dust exploded as she hit the bottom. Scrambling to her feet, she glared up at the boys and started back up the stairs. But then she saw the bandages spread across the stairs. The mummy woman looked down at her ancient body ... and clasped her arms together, trying to cover herself.

Owen saw his chance and ran across the landing. He scrabbled on the dusty carpet and found the finger. Picking it up, he raced towards an open window.

GARDEN GNOMES

It was a long way down.

But there was no other way.

Already the boys could hear the thud, thud, thud of the mummy woman on the stairs.

"Come on," yelled Owen, trying to hurry Freddie.

"Get a move on," said Chaz, climbing out onto the window ledge.

"Oi! Gerroff! Don't put your filthy, great foot in my ear'ole," said Freddie.

The boys climbed down as fast as they could, grabbing any hand-hold they could find. Chaz stuck to the ivy like a spider, while Owen slipped and slid his way down a drainpipe. Freddie seemed to be doing something from a PE lesson; he was upside down more often than he was the right way up. Owen was nearing the bottom when Chaz called out to him.

" 'Ere, are they garden gnomes down there?"

Owen stopped and looked down. The ground was covered with tiny figures. He blinked as he thought he could see several tiny horses pulling chariots.

"I'm sure they weren't there when we got here," called Chaz.

"Why are they holding those stick things?" said Freddie.

"Ouch!" yelped Owen. Something stung his leg. And then again.

Now Freddie and Chaz were yelping too. Below them, the little figures let fly a cloud of tiny spears. More figures were kneeling, aiming bows and arrows.

Trying to escape the spears and arrows, the boys started to climb back up. But then, the mummy's wife appeared at the open window above them. Opening her mouth wide, she let out a deafening screech. Something like a tornado shook the ivy on the walls so that the boys had to cling on tightly.

"What now?" shouted Chaz.

"How should I know?" Owen called back.

Just then, Freddie grabbed at a clump of ivy and the leaves came away in his hands. He found himself staring into an ugly face with bulging eyes. He saw it was only made of stone, but it was too late. He had already let go.

His fall was broken by a large, leafy bush and he scrambled out looking like a tree on legs. The tiny figures stepped back, afraid. Freddie saw their fear and he jumped up and down waving his arms and shouting.

"Yah, stupid gnomes. You can't get me."

Owen and Chaz saw their chance. They scrambled down and jumped the last few feet, landing heavily. But by now the tiny figures had grown braver. They began to advance on Freddie who stopped waving his arms. A few leaves fell to the ground.
He was just a boy again. The figures picked up their tiny weapons and came towards him.

Freddie gulped.

Suddenly, there was a rumbling sound. The first bowman turned and gave a cry of terror. Others turned and looked also. Coming towards them along the path rolled a great ball of stone like an enormous bowling ball. Several of the tiny figures leapt into the bushes to save themselves.

Owen looked at Chaz. "Did *you* throw that stone? Where did you learn to do that?"

"Oh, I did a bit of ten-pin-bowling with my dad, once," said Chaz, looking pleased with himself.

There was another scream from above. The mummy woman was coming down the ivy.

"Come on," said Owen. "Let's get out of here!"

DUMMIES

"This way," said Owen, "I think."

The map in his hand flapped like a bed sheet.

"If we head away from the river ... up here ... we should get back to the museum."

Owen stopped to look at the map. From somewhere behind them came a high-pitched scream.

"Come on, Owen," stammered Freddie, "we can't stop here."

"Not with Old Dusty Knickers after us," added Chaz.

With a hurried look at the map, Owen headed off down an empty side street.

The boys half-ran, half-walked, checking behind them all the while, expecting to see the mummy woman at any moment. Then, as they turned the next corner, a dark shape loomed out of the darkness. Freddie screamed. Owen felt a sharp stabbing pain in his ankle as he tumbled to the ground.

"Sorry mate, didn't see you there."

A boy in a crash helmet and knee pads clambered to his feet and picked up his skateboard.

"That's OK," replied Owen, sitting up and rubbing a bruised shin.

"Come on, Owen, stop messing about," said Freddie. "Let's get out of here."

Chaz watched the skateboarder sail off along the pavement, and then he bent down to help Owen up.

Just then, a deafening, high-pitched scream echoed against the walls, and the mummy woman came round the corner.

"Run!" yelled Chaz.

The others did not need to be told twice. Chaz and Freddie set off running. Owen limped along behind them, trying to keep up. The padded step of the mummy woman sounded behind them in the empty street.

Around the next corner, Owen stumbled.

"My ankle," he groaned.

"Don't stop now!" called out Freddie, horrified.

"You go on," said Owen, holding out the finger towards Chaz.

"Don't be nuts," said Chaz. "Quick! In here."

Chaz grabbed Owen's collar and pulled him into the nearest shop doorway. Freddie followed. As they bundled against the door, the handle gave way, and they fell in onto the floor. It was dark inside and there was no one about.

In a large window, several shop dummies stood, half-lit from the dim street light outside. One of the figures wore a long dress and had a large feather in her hat; another wore a cloak and had a mask over his eyes. The boys crept over and squeezed in next to the dummies. Chaz wiped away a circle of the dust from the window with his sleeve. They peered into the empty street. A tree branch scraped against the window and shadows moved on the wall opposite.

Suddenly the mummy woman was there, standing right outside the window. "Don't move," hissed Owen. "Pretend we're dummies."

"We must be dummies," whispered Chaz, "to let you get us into this mess!"

The mummy tipped back its head as if sniffing the air. Then it turned. And stared straight into the shop window. It tilted its head to one side, puzzled at the still figures staring back. Then, dropping its shoulders, the mummy woman shuffled away into the long shadows.

"'Ere, where's Freddie?" said Chaz.

Owen turned around, and screamed.

Staring back at him was the golden deathmask of an ancient Pharaoh.

FANCY THAT!

With a cry of terror, Owen lashed out. He caught the figure smack on the nose. His hand seemed to bounce off and the figure stumbled backwards.

"Ouch ... geroff ... whaddya-do-dat for?" it mumbled. The Pharaoh sat back heavily on the floor and peeled off a rubber mask.

63

"Freddie!" said Owen and Chaz together.

"What did you punch me on de nose for?" groaned Freddie.

"Well, what do you expect?" said Owen. "Where did you get that thing, anyway?"

Freddie dabbed at his nose with a tissue. With his other hand he pointed to a sign above his head.

**FANCY THAT
COSTUMES, FANCY DRESS
CLOSING DOWN SALE
EVERYTHING MUST GO**

"Wow! Look at all this stuff," said Chaz, pulling on a lion's head.

"Here ... try this on," said Freddie, holding out a bundle of yellow fluff.

"We haven't got time for this," said Owen, brushing the mask aside, "we've got to go."

Tip-toeing to the door, he peeped out into the light.

The street was silent.

He motioned the other boys to follow and stepped outside.

Following the map, the boys made their way along side streets and alleyways. They hurried across a deserted market, and passed a gloomy garden square behind railings. The boys crossed over, afraid of what may be hiding in the dark shadows. Then, around the next corner, they saw the museum.

The enormous stone building towered into the sky, tall pillars guarding a stone staircase. There was no one about. The boys approached the great iron gates. A heavy chain barred the way.

"How are we going to get in there?"

"That's not the worst problem," said Chaz. "Look!"

The boys peered into the courtyard. Something shifted and shimmered in the moonlight like black oil on the paving. Something that breathed and scuttled. Something alive!

"Scorpions!" breathed Owen.

"That's it. I'm off," said Freddie.

"Come on, Fred," said Chaz. "Don't give up on us now."

"Look, I've been speared by gnomes, chased by a mad mummy woman – and now you want me to be stung to death by scorpions?"

"...the death of a thousand stings," breathed Owen, staring through the railings. "How on earth are we going to get in there?"

"Bye," said Freddie, and he began to walk away.

"Hey, Fred," called Chaz. "Say hello to Old Dusty Knickers for me!"

"P'raps I'll stay ... just for a bit," muttered Freddie, shuffling back.

"Now," said Chaz, "I've got an idea."

Chaz climbed up onto the railings where several posters advertised the Egyptian exhibition. He began to untie one of them.

"What are you doing?" asked Freddie.

"You'll see," said Chaz. "Come on. Give me a hand."

Owen and Freddie climbed up and soon they had three bits of card on the ground. The posters were covered in a kind of plastic to protect them from the rain.

"I still don't get it!" said Freddie.

"Remember that skateboarder who we bumped into earlier?"

"But we've got no wheels," said Owen.

"Don't need any," grinned Chaz. "That's the best bit."

Further along, Chaz had noticed a hose pouring water into the gutter. He ran to it, holding a poster in one hand. He picked up the hose and pointed the jet through an old wooden gate. Chaz swung the hose from side-to-side, sending a spray of water whooshing into the courtyard. A few tails curved their deadly stings, but the scorpions stayed put.

The boys watched as Chaz now dropped the hose and took several paces backwards. Then, with a loud war cry, he charged at the gate... and disappeared from view. Owen and Freddie ran to the railings to see what was going on.

Chaz was surfing. Arms held wide, knees bent, Chaz skimmed over a sea of glistening shells.

"Yaaah! I'm skating on scorpions!" he yelled.

Freddie and Owen looked at each other and then copied Chaz and slid across the courtyard.

IN THE HALL OF THE EGYPTIANS

It was dark inside the museum.

A faint glimmer of moonlight spilled in from high windows.

Upstairs, in the Hall of the Egyptians, three shadows moved on the floor.

"'Ere, stop poking me!"

"Can't see where I'm going, can I?"

"Quiet! There might be guards," hissed Owen.

"Can't we just leave the finger here, somewhere?" suggested Freddie.

"How's the mummy s'posed to know it's here, cloth-brain?" said Owen.

"He knows, alright," snorted Chaz. "Who d'ya think sent his missus ... and those little archers?"

"*Shabti*," corrected Owen.

"Bless you," said Chaz.

"Sssh, what was that?" said Freddie.

From somewhere below them came a sound.

A door opening.

And footsteps.

The boys kept perfectly still, hardly daring to breathe. There was no mistaking the sound. A muffled padding. And it was coming their way.

"What are we going to do?" stammered Freddie.

"Hide!" hissed Chaz.

"Where? There's only glass cases in here ... and they're full of mummies!"

"Look, by the wall," said Owen, "those jars."

"But isn't that where they keep the mummy's ... guts and stuff?"

"Yes, but not now," said Owen, though he was not altogether sure.

The boys hurried over, trying not to make any noise. The jars were nearly as tall as them and each had a lid in the shape of an animal head. Chaz lifted off the first one and scrambled in. When he stood up, his head just poked out of the top. Freddie and Owen did the same.

"I can't reach the lid," said Owen.

"He'll see us," said Freddie.

"Here put these on. I got them from that shop," said Chaz.

Owen felt something rubbery pushed

into his hand.

He listened as the footsteps sounded again, closer now ... step ... shuffle ... step. He peered into the dark, trying to make out a shape in the blackness. In his imagination Owen could see the bandaged figure coming ... step ... shuffle ... step ... dragging one leg across the ground.

Then it stopped.

Silence.

And then another sound.

Breathing.

A wheezing, choking breath.

And a sharp smell, like rotting meat.

And the footsteps began again. Coming this way. But there was another sound now. A steady, more even step this time ... pad ... pad ... pad ....

Owen realised his eyes were shut tight.

When he opened them he wanted to scream.

He was staring at the back of a bandaged head.

Slowly, the head turned until it was looking directly at him. Empty eye-sockets like two black holes.

The mummy tilted its head to one side, trying to work something out. Somewhere in this room was his missing finger.

Chum Ra Otep had been awakened from the sleep of a thousand years. He had tried to scratch his nose. That was when he had counted his fingers. He had never been very good with Egyptian numbers, but he could count to four.

In a boiling rage, the pharaoh had sent his warriors to seek out the ones who dared to steal the royal finger. And now the grave-robbers were here – somewhere in this room.

He shuffled back again, past the line of clay jars. Once these jars had held his heart, his liver, his stomach, but they were empty now. The heads of the gods stood watch like old friends. Here was Sekhmet, the lion. And Ra the sun god, a pharaoh, like himself. He shuffled to the next in line. And here ... a fluffy duck?

He peered closer at the yellow feathers and the grinning beak. He peered into the creature's round eyes. He wished he had listened better at school. He could not remember a god with the head of a yellow duck.

A gust of wind blew in from an open window. A feather escaped from the duck's fluffy head.

The mummy frowned. Its lip curled. A low sound, like the snarl of a jungle cat, gurgled in its throat.

The feather drifted down on the cold air, and settled ...

... on Fluffy Duck's nose.

Owen sneezed.

THE MUMMY'S FINGER

Then everything happened at once.

Owen tried to put a hand to his face to stop another sneeze. He forgot his hands were trapped inside the narrow jar. He could feel the jar tipping and he struggled to keep himself upright. But that was hopeless. The jar toppled sideways, banging into the next one, and the next. Now the jars were falling like dominoes.

"What's going on?" yelled Chaz.

"Help, I'm falling!"came Freddie's voice.

There was a sound like someone throwing plates. The boys tumbled onto the floor. Owen looked up from among the pieces of broken jar. There was the mummy of Chum Ra Otep. It tipped back its head and let out a roar which shook the glass cabinets all around.

"Run!" shouted Chaz.

No-one argued. They scrambled up, slipping over broken pottery, and headed off down the long room, dodging in and out of the glass cabinets. At the end was a huge pillar covered in Egyptian writing.

"Quick, behind here," said Owen. The boys pressed themselves against the stone and waited. The sound of footsteps could soon be heard, echoing from the stone floor.

"Don't make a sound," whispered Owen.

And there, on the other side of the pillar, was a low rumble, like thunder. And the hot stink of the mummy's breath.

Freddie and Chaz looked, wide-eyed, at Owen. Next to them was a cabinet with a wooden boat inside. Owen peered hard into the glass. A dark shape moved across it... the reflection of the mummy coming round the pillar.

Owen pointed. "This way."

The boys edged around, their backs
against the cold stone. Owen watched the
reflection in the glass. The mummy was close
behind.

"When I say run ... RUN!"

The boys set off as fast as they could, back down the hall. A cry of rage echoed behind them. At the end of the hall was a cross-roads. Four different stairways led off to more hallways.

"Which way?" said Chaz.

"Not this one," said Freddie. "Look!"

With a hissing, scuttling sound, the floor began to flood with shiny, black shapes.

"Scorpions!" said Freddie.

"This way's no good, neither," said Chaz.

An army of tiny figures was coming towards them carrying spears and bows and arrows.

"This way, then," said Owen. He stepped onto the staircase, but stopped in his tracks as a terrifying scream echoed from the walls. From behind a stone coffin stepped a bandaged figure. Wisps of hair escaped from under the bandaged head. A sandy handbag dangled from one arm.

"Back, the other way," yelled Owen.

But as they turned, the mummy of Chum Ra Otep was already coming towards them, staggering up the stairs. The boys tried to go in three directions all at once. Banging into each other, Freddie and Chaz only succeeded in knocking Owen off the top step.

Owen looked down in horror as he fell.

Chum Ra Otep raised his head. A boy was falling towards him.

The mummy stretched out his left arm. His cracked mouth broke into something like a grin.

Owen put out both hands to save himself, one of them still clutching the mummy's finger.

He felt it slipping ... slipping away from him.

And then, for a moment, Owen and the mummy's hands met. There was a wet, sucking noise, like jelly being scooped up from a bowl with a spoon ... and then Owen landed on the hard floor.

* * * * *

"What on earth's going on?"

Torches swept the floor. And then a light flicked on and the boys blinked at the brightness.

Two men in blue uniforms stood eyeing the boys curiously.

"How did you get in here?"

"Er ... we were on our school outing," began Chaz, "and we got lost ..."

"Yes, that's right," added Freddie. "Must have got locked in ..."

Owen stood up and looked around him.

On one side was a glass case with a

handful of tiny clay statues, all warriors. Nearby, a single black-wood scorpion sat on its own stone column. At the far end of the room were the mummies. Even from here he could see the open coffins of the pharaoh and his bride. And there, in his own glass case, was Chum Ra Otep, himself.

Owen hurried over. An ancient body, perfectly preserved. You could make out every feature under the thin bandages: hair, eyes, nose ... mouth slightly open, almost a smile.

Two arms folded across a royal chest. Hands laid neatly. Fingers outstretched so you could count them, every single one.

One, two, three, four, five, six, seven, eight, nine ...

Ten!

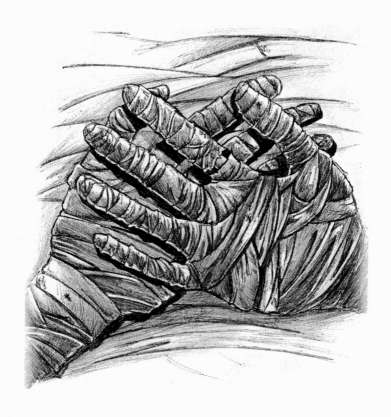

Also available from

PUBLISHING

Eyeball Soup by Ian MacDonald
ISBN 978-1-904904-59-9

Here are two amazing sci-fi stories in one book! Told with
generous helpings of excitement, adventure and humour, Eyeball
Soup and Magut the Alien are bound to appeal to young readers
and especially boys.

Alien Teeth by Ian MacDonald
ISBN 978-1-905637-32-4
Selected for the SLA Boys into Books (5-11) 2008 List.

When you accidentally sit on a set of teeth, they can be hard to
remove from your bottom ... especially when they belong to an
alien who left them behind on a flying visit to Earth. The
precious molars belong to Emperor Zarg and he wants them
back!

Chip McGraw by Ian MacDonald
ISBN 978-1-905637-08-9

Chip McGraw is the toughest cowboy in the West. He drinks
lemonade from a dirty glass ... and he doesn't even carry a gun.
Bradley McIntire has two heroes in his life: his dad and Chip
McGraw. But when burglars turn up at the school disco, is it Dad
... or Chip McGraw who saves the day?

Skateboard Gran by Ian MacDonald
ISBN 978-1-905637-30-0

Tom is very sensible; his Gran, on the other hand, is completely bonkers! When Tom finds himself in a spot of financial bother, the prize in a skateboard competition seems to be the answer. The only problem is that he is too scared to skateboard! He is delighted when Gran offers to enter the competition, until she has an accident on her board. Then Tom has to face his own fears ... and ride the terrifying 'Wall of Death'...

Sam's Spitfire Summer by Ian MacDonald
ISBN 978-1-905637-43-0

When Sam is evacuated, he might as well be going to the moon. Ten-year-old Sam watches the familiar sights of London disappear in a cloud of steam as he sets off on a journey to the unfamiliar world of country cottages, farmyard animals and a hostile welcome at the village school.

The Magician's Bag by Ian MacDonald
ISBN 978-1-905637-60-7

When two bags are accidentally swapped at a train station, strange things start to happen to Seb. Disembodied voices echo in train carriages, pencils leap inside bottles and a white rabbit disrupts a school football match. Inside the bag Seb finds a map that will lead him to an Egyptian necklace. But someone else is on the trail too - the owner of the magic bag who plans to steal the precious necklace!

Porky Pies by Suzi Cresswell
ISBN 978-1-905637-66-9

Jaz has a bad habit - he can't stop telling little white lies. When he joins a new school, he tells his classmates that he's the son of pop star Rocky Riff. Jaz finds himself in big trouble when Aisha turns out to be his greatest fan and Clint demands proof...

Jade Fry, Private Eye by Suzi Cresswell
ISBN 978-1-905637-75-1

Jade is fed up when she has to stay with her Gran. But life there is more exciting than expected as she is soon swept up in an exciting adventure involving Gran's pony, Captain. Captain is important to Gran's friend, a race horse trainer whose star horse, Smithy, is due to run in the Melton Chase soon. Without Captain, Smithy won't get into the horse box. But it seems that someone wants to stop him competing when Captain disappears. Jade turns detective and tries to find out what is going on...

The Library Ghost by David Webb
ISBN 978-1-904374-66-4

It's a Victorian day at Mill Street School to help raise money for a new library! Children and staff are all dressed up in Victorian costume. All except for the sneering spoilsport, Delia Grime, that is. All goes well until Delia causes chaos at the coffee afternoon, trying to kidnap a valuable Victorian china doll. However, she's in for a ghostly shock when she makes her escape to the old school library!

Professor Nutter and the Curse of the Pharaoh's Tomb
by David Webb   ISBN 978-1-905637-42-3

When Professor Nutter finds an old map hidden in a secret room, it is the start of an amazing adventure. The map shows the site of an undiscovered Pharaoh's tomb. The Professor and his nephew travel to Egypt in search of the secret burial place. Will they fall victim to the curse of the Pharaoh's tomb?

Professor Nutter and the Gladiator's Ghost
by David Webb   ISBN 978-1-905637-59-1

When Professor Nutter and his nephew Nigel camp out on the moors, they are awoken in the night by ghostly sounds. Through the swirling mist they see a legion of Roman soldiers marching along the road. However, when they are confronted by the gladiator's ghost, it is the start of a journey back in time to the greatest theatre of all...

Friday the Thirteenth by David Webb
ISBN 978-1-905637-37-9

On Friday the 13th, Callum has to walk to school in the freezing cold, as he's been held up by his annoying sister. Things get even worse when he arrives at school late to face his strict new teacher who makes him look after the dreadful Daisy, a new girl. However, Callum rises to the challenge when the school computers are stolen and Friday the thirteenth turns into his lucky day!

Beastly Things in the Barn by Sandra Glover
ISBN 978-1-905637-75-1

Farmer's son Mark is delighted when they manage to rent their newly converted barn to a family for the summer. But Mark's delight turns to horror when the Beesley-Trings, quickly renamed the Beastly Things, arrive. They are completely mad and even worse, they seem determined to ruin Mark's life. Still, it's only for six weeks, so it can't be that bad...or can it?

The Crash by Sandra Glover
ISBN 978-1-905637-29-4

A plane has come down in a field near Sam's farm but, with the arrival of the armed forces, it becomes clear that this is no ordinary crash. Just what is the secretive Major Parker hiding? And why is Sam's family being kept in the house, with all communication cut off?

Deadline by Sandra Glover
ISBN 978-1-904904-30-4

Ten-year-old Scott isn't really interested in the school newspaper but his best friend Joss is determined that they are going to be crime reporters. What's more, Joss thinks he has the perfect story to investigate; the case of his neighbour's missing gnome! Along the way the pair incur the wrath of their parents, the police, raiders and even worse, their teacher.

Order online @ **www.eprint.co.uk**